Brandon Makes Jiǎo Zi (餃子)

EUGENIA CHU

ILLUSTRATED BY HELENA CHU HO

Outskirts Press, Inc.
http://www.outskirtspress.com

Paperback ISBN: 978-1-4787-7408-2
Hardback ISBN: 978-1-4787-9038-9

Illustrated by: Helena Chu Ho. All rights reserved - used with permission.

Outskirts Press and the "OP" logo are trademarks belonging to Outskirts Press, Inc.

PRINTED IN THE UNITED STATES OF AMERICA

THIS BOOK BELONGS TO:

Preface

This book contains a few words and phrases written in Chinese characters and spelled in Pinyin.

Unlike English (and other Roman-based languages) writing where each letter in each word represents a sound, Chinese writing evolved from pictures and symbols. Chinese characters represent words and do not constitute an alphabet or represent sounds. Accordingly, Pinyin is often used by those learning Chinese.

Pinyin is the official system to transcribe Mandarin Chinese sounds into the Roman alphabet. It was invented in the 1950s, and adopted as a standard in mainland China in 1958. Pinyin assigns letters different sounds. For example:

ai is pronounced as i in like
ao is pronounced as ow in how
iao is pronounced as eow in meow
iang is pronounced as young
ie is pronounced as ye in yes
iu is pronounced as yo in yolk
ui is pronounced as way

In addition, in Mandarin Chinese there are four basic tones and a fifth neutral tone. Each syllable in each word has one of these tones. Changing the tone of a word changes its meaning. You can tell which tone to give a syllable by the marks above the vowels in pinyin (ˉ ´ ˇ `).

The first tone is high and remains level. It is represented by :

The second tone goes up and is abrupt. It is represented by :

The third tone falls in pitch and then goes up again. It is represented by :

The fourth tone falls in pitch from a high to a low level. It is represented by :

There is also a neutral (or toneless) tone, which is pronounced weakly. The neutral tone has no mark above the vowel.

Chinese is a fun language to learn! I hope you and your child will enjoy reading this story as much as I have enjoyed writing it.

This is Brandon. Brandon is a smart but silly boy.

Brandon loves jiǎo zi (餃子), which are Chinese dumplings. Brandon loves to make jiǎo zi (餃子) and he really loves to EAT them!

One day after school, Mommy had a surprise for him in the car. It was Pó Po (婆婆), Brandon's grandma visiting from China! Brandon was so excited to see her! He couldn't stop laughing and talking the whole ride home from school.

When Brandon got home and went to the kitchen for a snack, he saw flour and dough on a huge cutting board next to a big bowl on the table. Brandon started jumping up and down! He looked at Pó Po (婆婆) and excitedly asked, "Pó Po (婆婆), are we going to make jiǎo zi (餃子)?" Pó Po (婆婆) responded, "Duì le (對了)!"—which means that's right in Chinese. Brandon started to do his happy dance!

Brandon then ran to the bathroom to wash his hands while Pó Po (婆婆) started rolling out the dough to prepare the jiǎo zi (餃子) wraps. Once Brandon's hands were nice and clean, he sat down next to Pó Po (婆婆), looked around and decided, "We need more flour." And before Pó Po (婆婆) could stop him, Brandon grabbed the nearby flour bag to sprinkle flour on the table. But instead of a light sprinkling of flour, a mountain of flour came crashing down on the table and got everywhere! Including all over Brandon! It was even in his hair!

Pó Po (婆婆) couldn't help but laugh! "Aì yà! Nǐ hǎo xiàng xiǎo guǐ (你好像小鬼)!"—you look like a little ghost! Brandon started to smile and suddenly jumped up and yelled "BOO!" Pó Po (婆婆) and Brandon couldn't stop laughing!

Once Brandon and Pó Po (婆婆) finally settled down and cleaned up, they got to work. Brandon started spooning in the meat mixture from the big bowl into the wraps. He then pinched the edges together to keep all the delicious filling inside. He loved making jiǎo zi (餃 子) and was getting really good at it!

Pó Po (婆婆) looked over and exclaimed, "Wā, Brandon, nǐ zuò de jiǎo zi zhēn piào liàng (你做的餃子真漂亮)!"—saying that Brandon was making beautiful dumplings! Brandon was very proud!

Once they had a tray full of jiǎo zi (餃子) prepared, Pó Po (婆婆) started to cook them while Brandon continued making more jiǎo zi (餃子). Soon all the dough and meat were used up and the first batch of jiǎo zi (餃子) was done! Brandon could not wait to eat them and his mouth started to water!

Pó Po (婆婆) asked Brandon, "Nǐ yào chī jí ge jiǎo zi (你要吃幾個餃子)?"—how many dumplings do you want to eat? Brandon replied, "ten—shí ge (十個)!" "Wā (哇)!" Pó Po (婆婆) cried, "Shí ge (十個)! Nǐ kě bū kě yǐ chī zhè me duō (你可不可以吃這麼多)?"—can you eat that many? Brandon started laughing and answered, "Yes, yes I can!" So, Pó Po (婆婆) gave him ten jiǎo zi (餃子) and Brandon counted them out one by one in Chinese—"yī, èr, sān, sì, wǔ, liù, qī, bā, jiǔ, shí (一二三四五六七八九十)—good they are all here!"

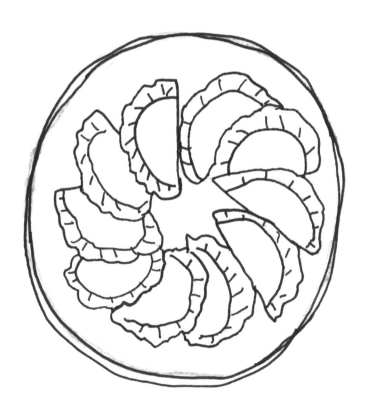

Then Brandon started eating!

And eating . . .

and eating!

Soon all ten jiǎo zi (餃子) were in Brandon's tummy! And his tummy was very big indeed!

Pó Po (婆婆) couldn't believe Brandon ate so many jiǎo zi (餃子) so quickly! "Wā! Nǐ tài bǎo le (你太飽了)!"—you must be too full! Brandon giggled and said, "They were so good I couldn't stop eating! I would like one more, please." Pó Po (婆婆) couldn't believe it! "Nǐ hái yào yí ge jiǎo zi (你還要一個餃子)?!?"—you want one more dumpling?!? Brandon laughed and said "Yes, please." So, Pó Po (婆婆) gave Brandon one more jiǎo zi (餃子) and watched, expecting him to eat it. But instead of eating the jiǎo zi (餃子), Brandon put it in a little box and said, "xiè xie (謝謝)"—thank you. Pó Po (婆婆) laughed and said, "What are you going to do with that jiǎo zi (餃子)? I thought you were going to eat it!" Brandon just smiled and said, "I want to save it because it is so beautiful."

Later, when everyone was busy, Brandon snuck out his jiǎo zi (餃子), took it out of the box and started to decorate it with strips of lettuce for hair, sliced olives for eyes, a piece of grape for the nose and a little slice of red pepper for the mouth! He stuck everything on with a little oyster sauce and called everyone in to see his masterpiece!

Mommy, Daddy, Pó Po (婆婆) and Gōng Gong (公公) (Brandon's grandpa) were so surprised and delighted by Brandon's creation! There were lots of oohs and ahhs and ai yos! Brandon took a picture of his little jiǎo zi (餃子) guy and then ate it all up in two bites! "Yummy hǎo chī (好吃)!" Everyone laughed and laughed. Brandon laughed the loudest.

What a smart but silly boy!